WHO WANTS
Arthur?

Library of Congress Cataloging-in-Publication Data

Graham, Amanda, 1961-
   Who wants Arthur?

   (A Quality time book)
   Rev. ed. of: Who Wants Arthur
   Summary: Arthur, a dog in a pet store waiting to be
adopted, takes on the identities of other animals he
thinks might be more appealing, until discovering that
he can be a success as himself.
   [1. Dogs—Fiction. 2. Pets—Fiction. 3. Individuality—
Fiction] I. Gynell, Donna, ill. II. Graham, Amanda, 1961-   .
Arthur. III. Title.
PZ7.G751664Wh 1987 [E]   88-42959
ISBN 1-55532-868-7 (lib. bdg.)
ISBN 1-55532-893-8 (Big Book)
ISBN 1-55532-943-8 (Soft-cover)

North American edition first published in 1987 by

Gareth Stevens Children's Books
RiverCenter Building, Suite 201
1555 North RiverCenter Drive
Milwaukee, Wisconsin   53212, USA

Text copyright © 1984 by Amanda Graham
Illustrations copyright © 1984 by Donna Gynell

First published in Australia as *Arthur* by ERA Publications

Printed in the United States of America

3 4 5 6 7 8 9 96 95 94 93 92 91 90

WHO WANTS
Arthur?

Story by Amanda Graham   Pictures by Donna Gynell

Gareth Stevens Publishing
Milwaukee

Arthur was a very ordinary dog.

He lived in Mrs. Humber's Pet Shop
with many other animals.
But Arthur was the only dog.
All the other dogs had been sold
because dogs were very popular —
all the dogs except Arthur.

He was just an ordinary brown dog,
who dearly wanted a home,
with a pair of old slippers to chew.

On Monday morning,
Mrs. Humber put some rabbits
in the window.

By the end of the day,
the window was empty —
except for Arthur.

Nobody wanted an ordinary brown dog.
Everybody wanted rabbits.

So that night,
when all was quiet,
Arthur practiced being a rabbit.

He practiced eating carrots
and poking out his front teeth
and making his ears stand up straight.

He practiced very hard
until he was sure
he could be a rabbit.

The next morning,
Mrs. Humber put some snakes in the window.

By the end of the day,
the window was empty —
except for Arthur.

Nobody wanted an ordinary brown dog,
not even one who acted like a rabbit.
Everybody wanted snakes.

So that night,
when all was quiet,
Arthur practiced being a snake.

He practiced

h i s s i n g

and *slithering*

and sliding

and looking cool.

He practiced very hard,
until he was sure
he could be a snake.

The next morning,
Mrs. Humber put some fish in the window.

By the end of the day,
the window was empty —
except for Arthur.

Nobody wanted an ordinary brown dog,
not even one who acted
like a rabbit
and a snake.
Everybody wanted a fish.

So that night,
when all was quiet,
Arthur practiced being a fish.

He practiced swimming
and blowing bubbles
and breathing underwater.

He practiced very hard,
until he was sure
he could be a fish.

The next morning,
Mrs. Humber put some cats in the window.

By the end of the day,
the window was empty —
except for Arthur.

Nobody wanted an ordinary brown dog,
not even one who acted
like a rabbit
and a snake
and a fish.
Everybody wanted cats.

Arthur felt he would never find a home
with a pair of old slippers to chew.

The next morning,
Mrs. Humber put the rest of her pets in the window.

There were two hamsters,
a cage of mice, three canaries,
a blue parakeet, a green frog,
one sleepy lizard,
and Arthur.

Arthur jumped on lilypads,
squeaked and nibbled cheese,
purred, croaked,
and even tried to fly.

By the end of the day,
the window was empty —
except for Arthur.

He had collapsed,
exhausted,
in the corner of the window.

Now he was certain
he would never find a home,
whether he was
a rabbit,
a snake,
a fish,
a cat,
or a purple, spotted, three-headed donkey.

Arthur decided that he might as well
be just an ordinary brown dog.

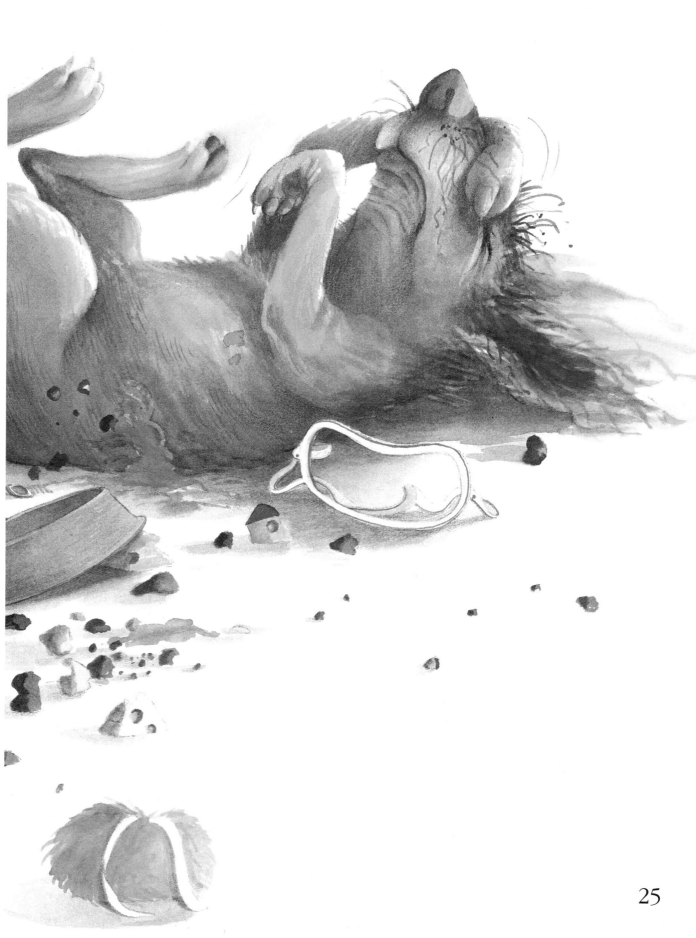

Late that afternoon,
as Mrs. Humber
was closing the shop,
a man came in with
his granddaughter.
"Excuse me," he said.
"Melanie tells me that
you have a rather
extraordinary dog
who performs
all sorts of tricks."

"The only dog I have,"
replied Mrs. Humber,
"is Arthur."

26

"There he is, Grandpa,
in the window!" cried Melanie.

She rushed to pick up Arthur,
who gave her the biggest,
wettest, doggiest
lick ever.

At last!
Arthur knew he had found a home,

with a pair of old slippers to chew.